MW01070743

Gracie Meets a Ghost

Keiko Sena

MUSEYON, New York

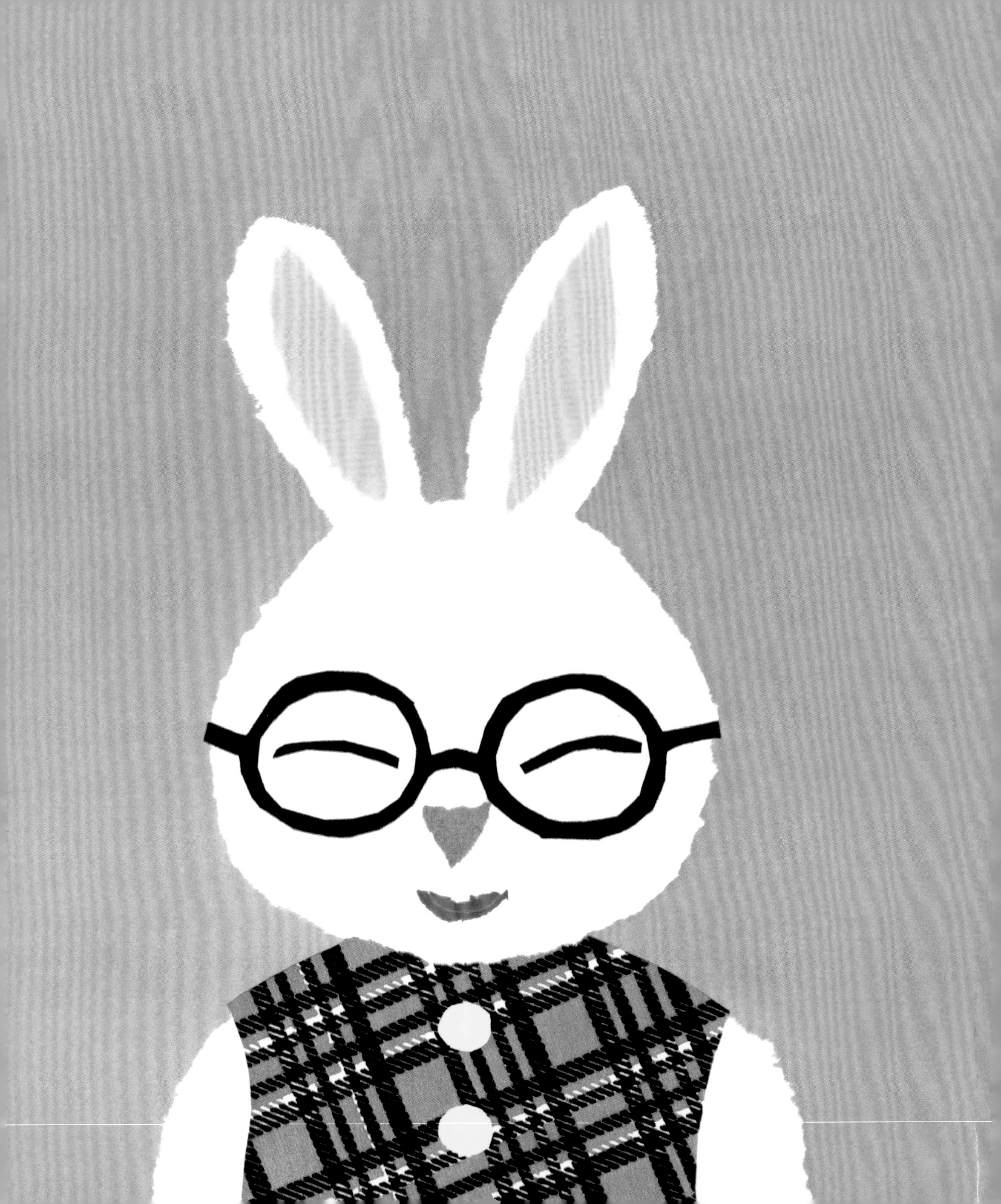

Gracie was having a hard time seeing clearly.

She loved reading books,
but the letters looked blurry.
So she bought a pair of glasses.

"Gracie wears glasses," her friends teased.
She was a little embarrassed,
but she was a little proud too.

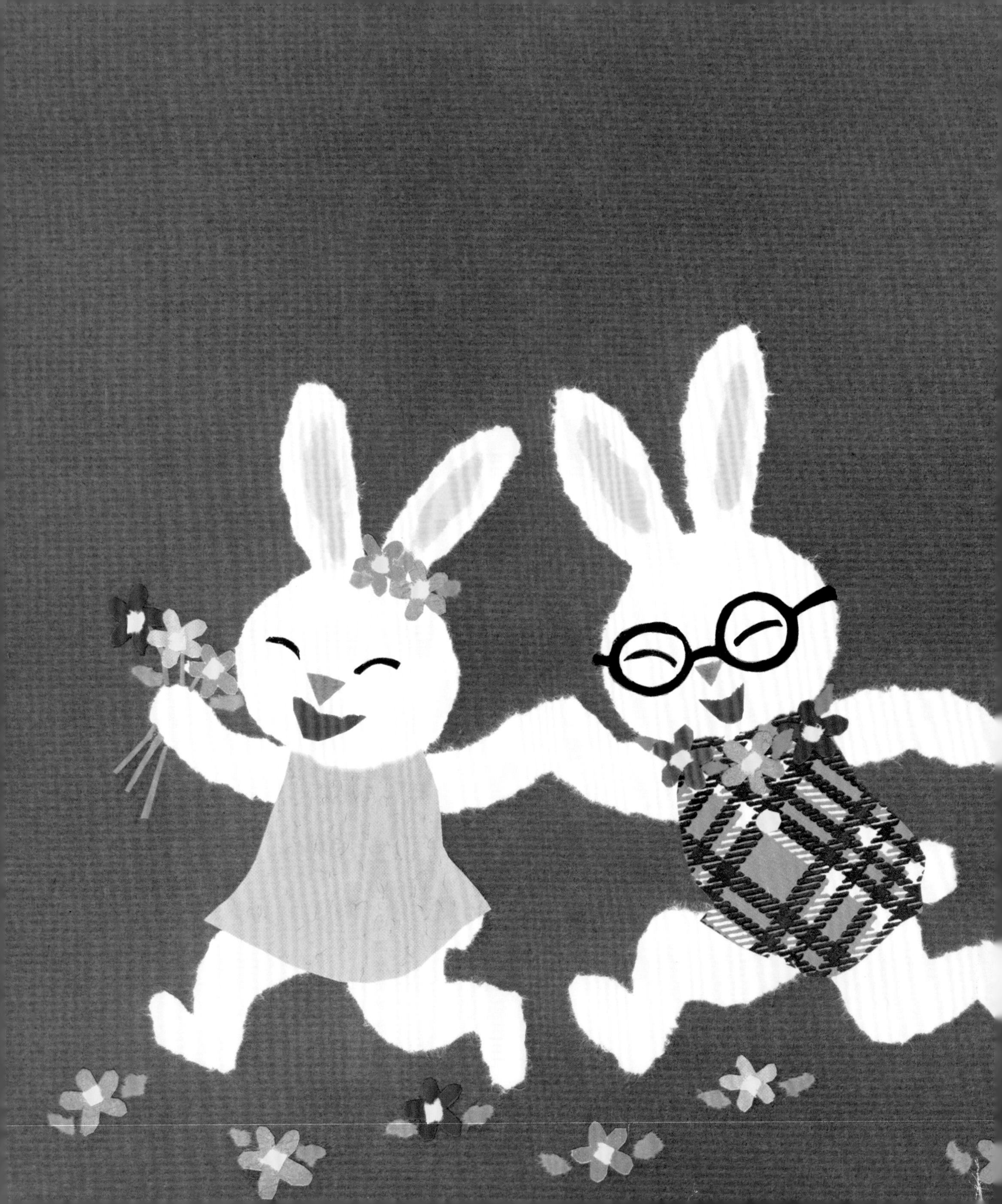

One day, Gracie and her friends went up the mountain to play.

They picked flowers,
danced around,
and had lots of fun, but . . .

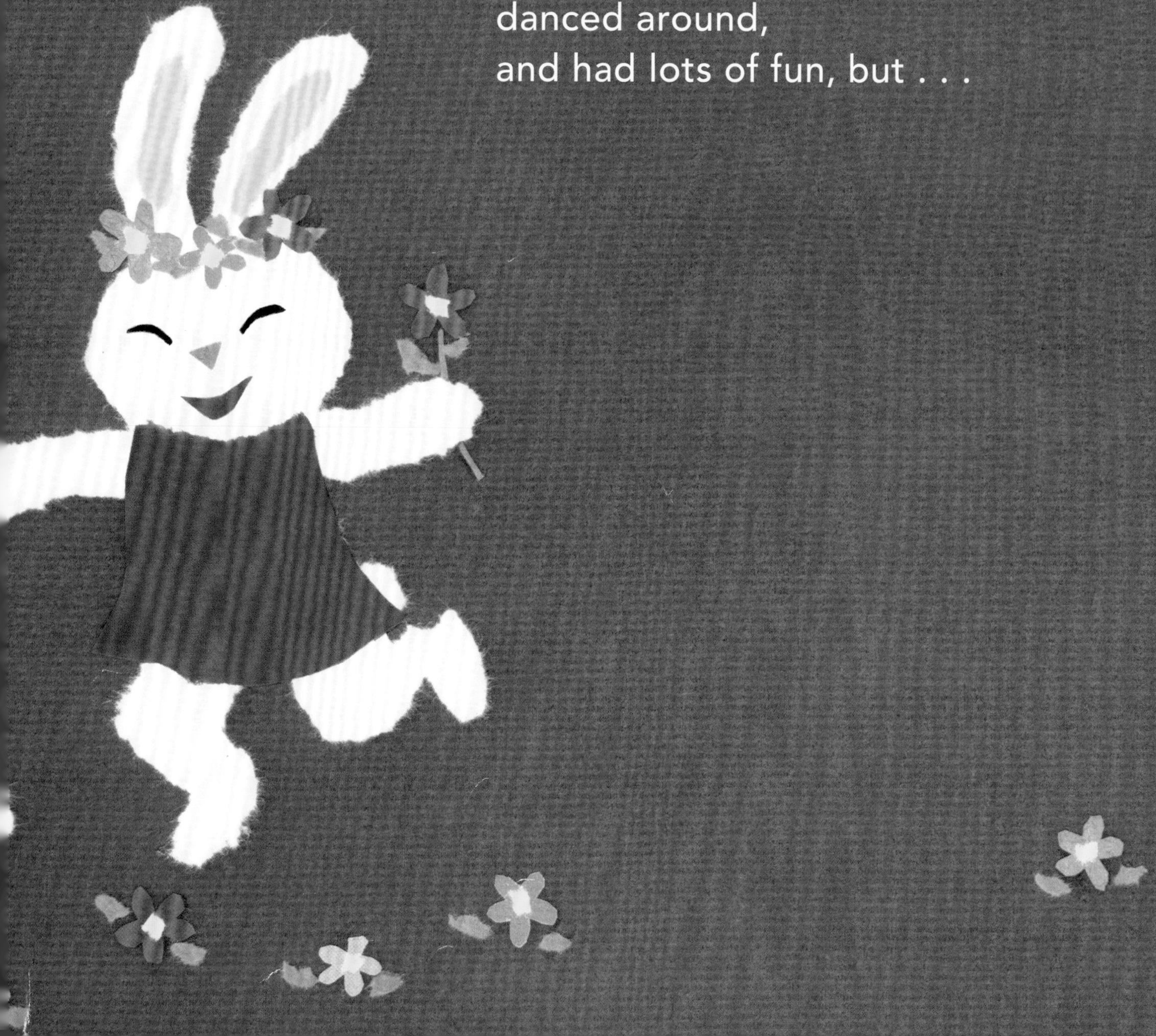

That night, when Gracie went to bed,
she tried to take off her glasses.

Oops!

She realized that
she wasn't wearing them!

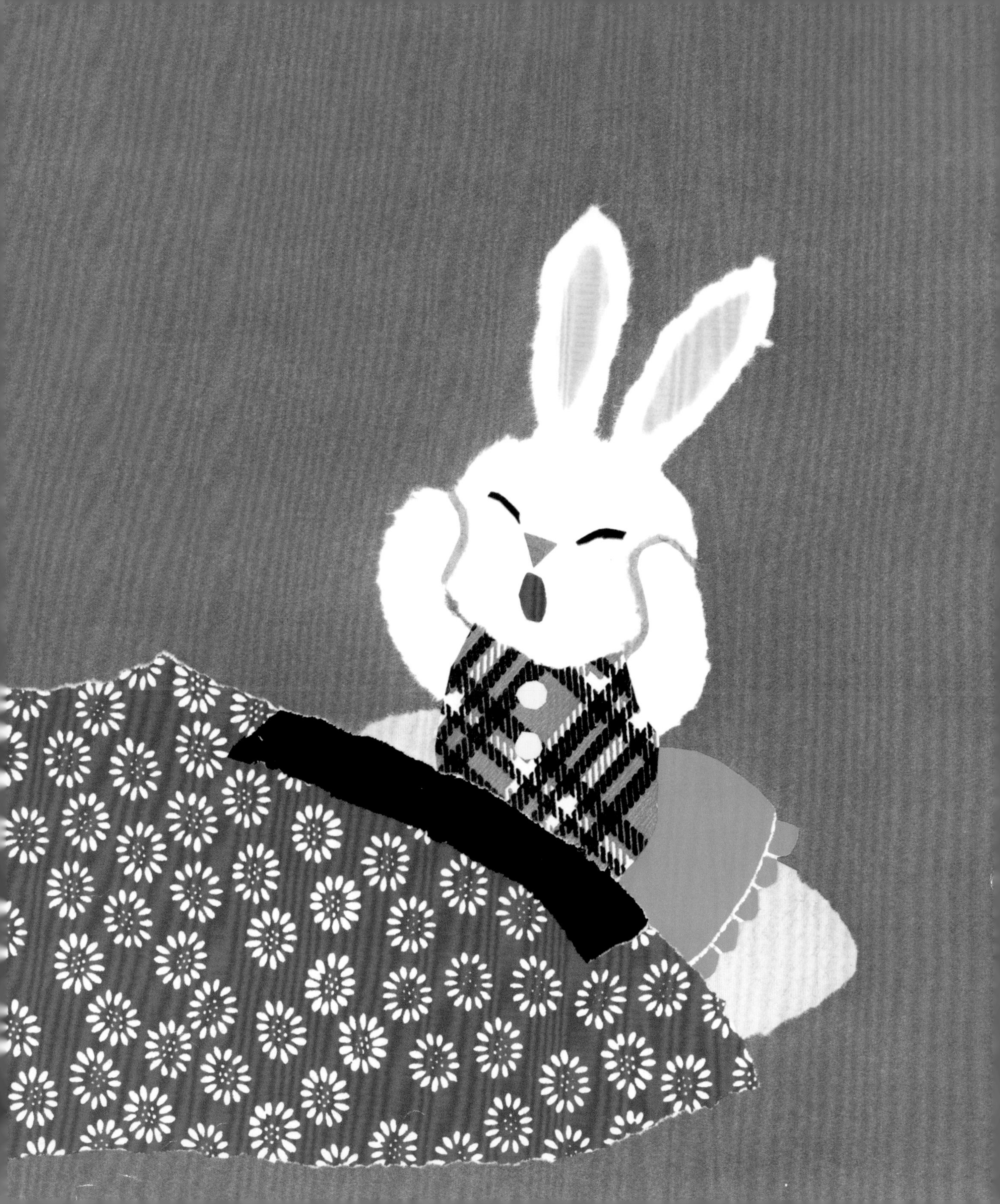

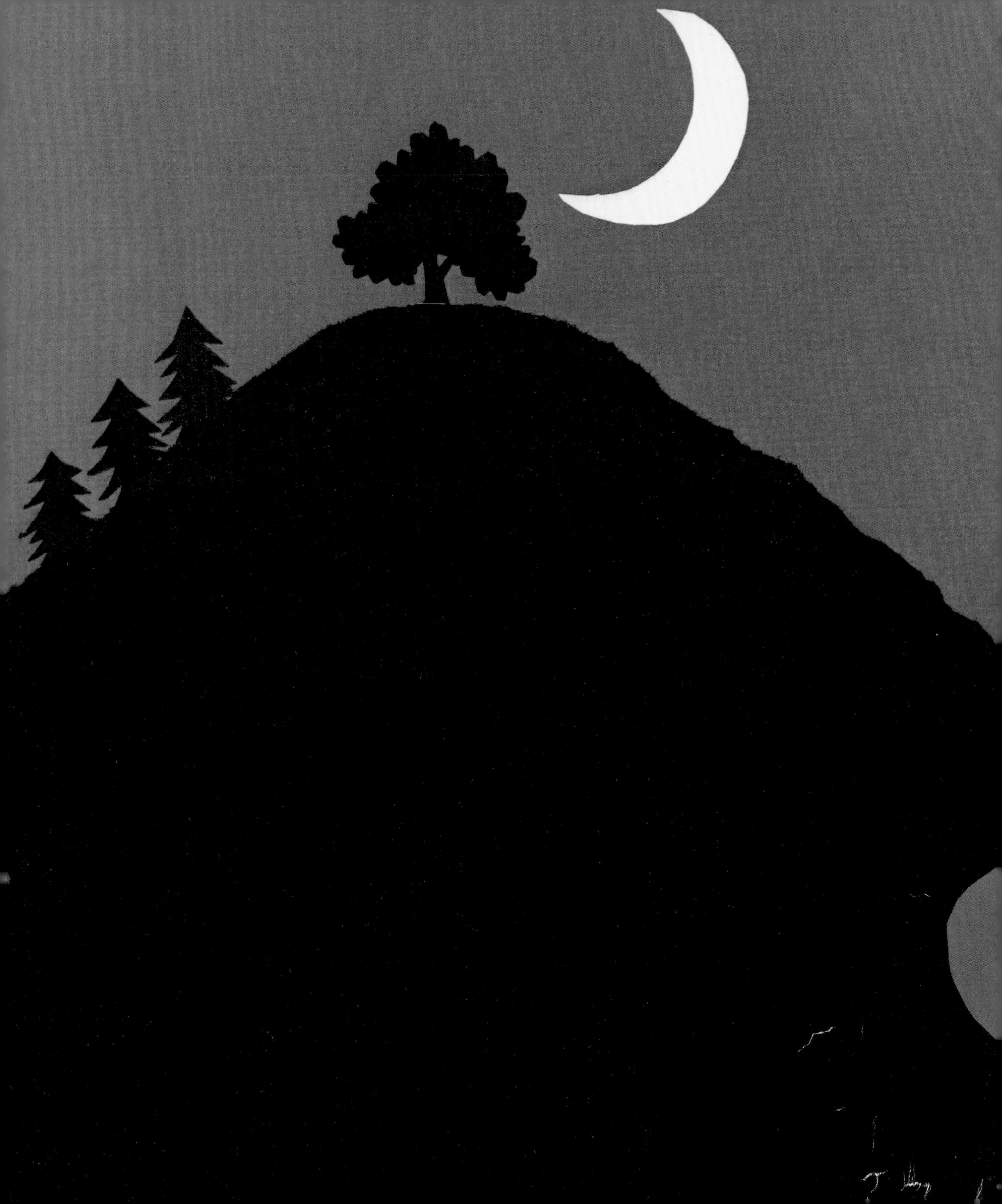

I must have dropped them on the mountain, she thought. *That's okay. I know the mountain paths. I will go back and look for them now.*

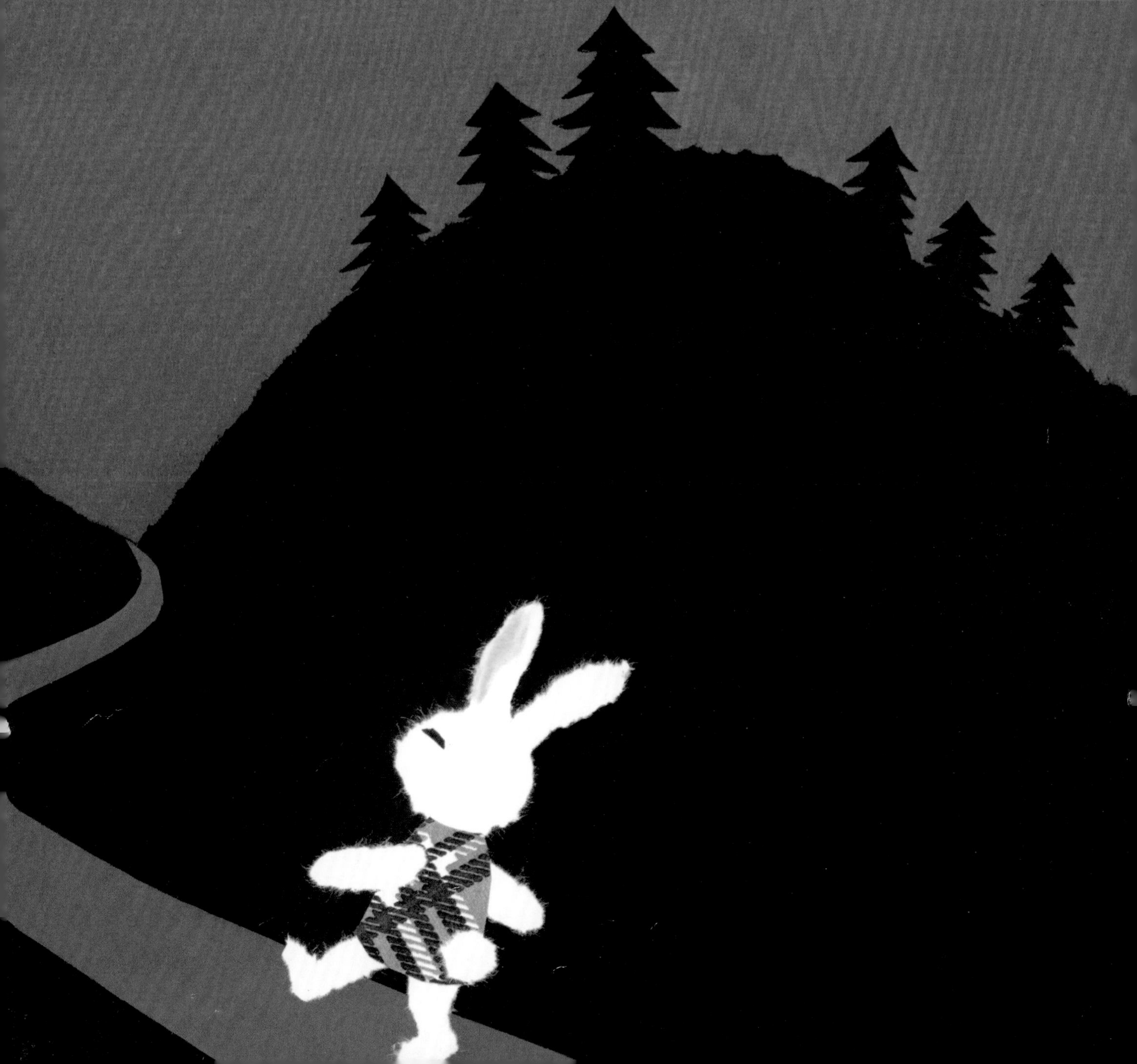

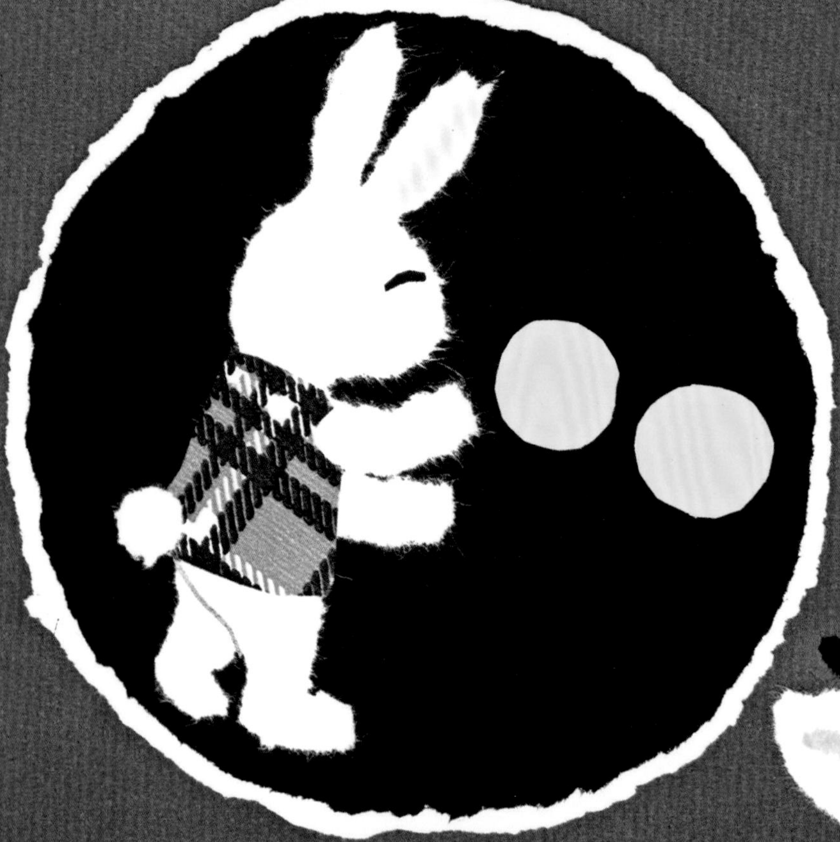

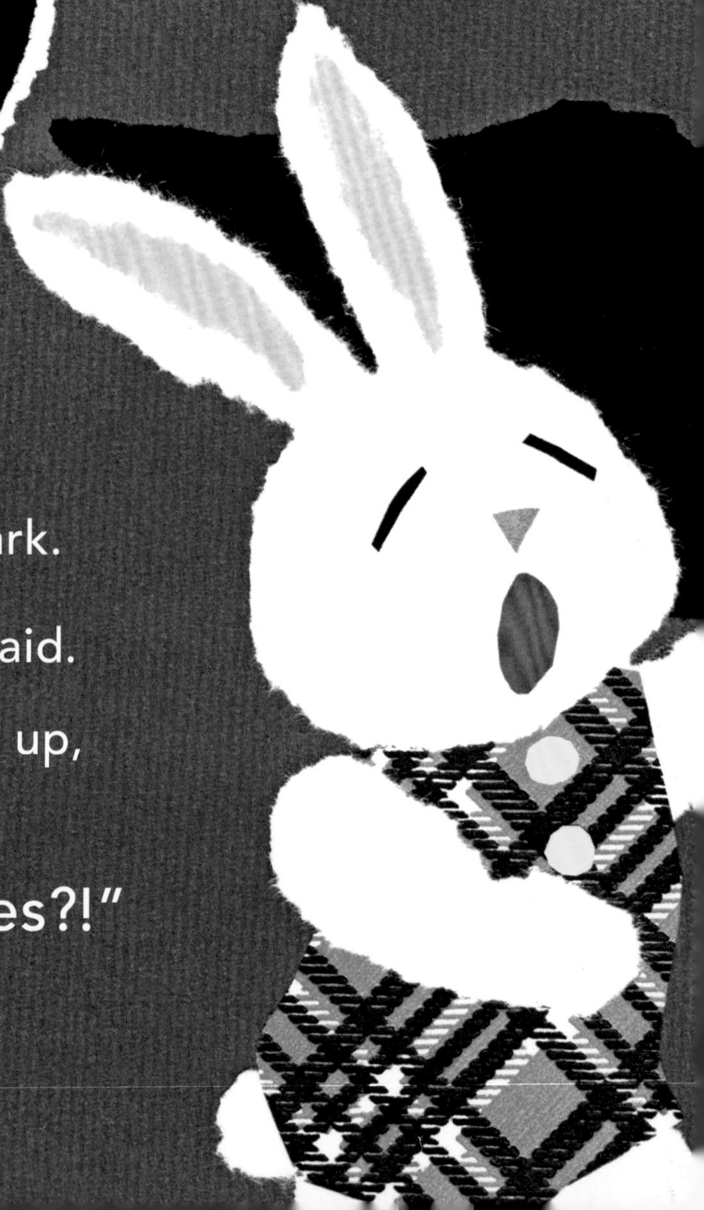

On the mountain, Gracie saw
a pair of lenses shining in the dark.

"Ah! I found them!" she said.

But when she tried to pick them up,
she heard a voice.

"Whooo is poking my eyes?!"

It was an owl!
What had looked like Gracie's glasses was really the owl's eyes.

"I'm so sorry. I thought those were my glasses," said Gracie.

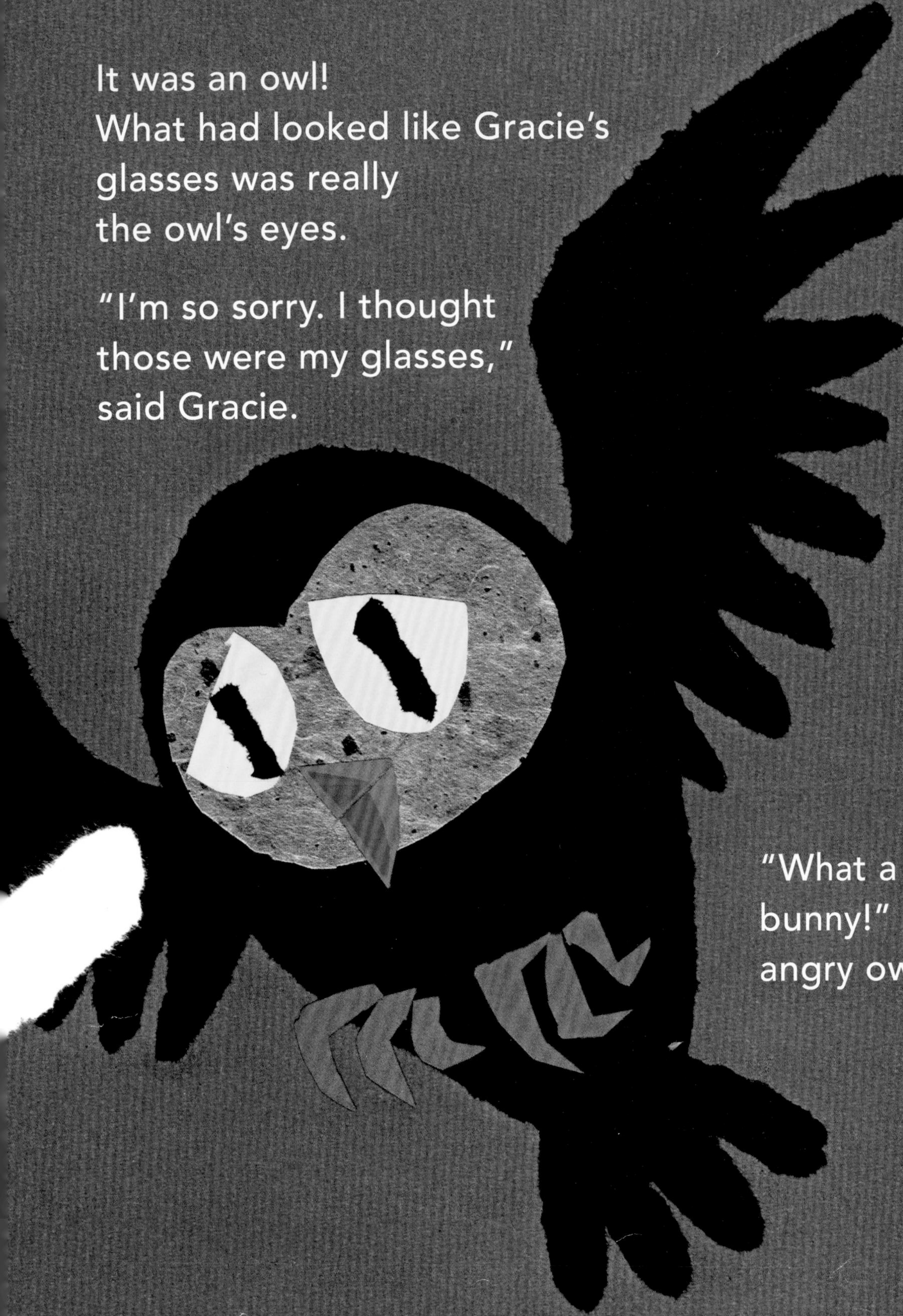

"What a rooooood bunny!" said the angry owl.

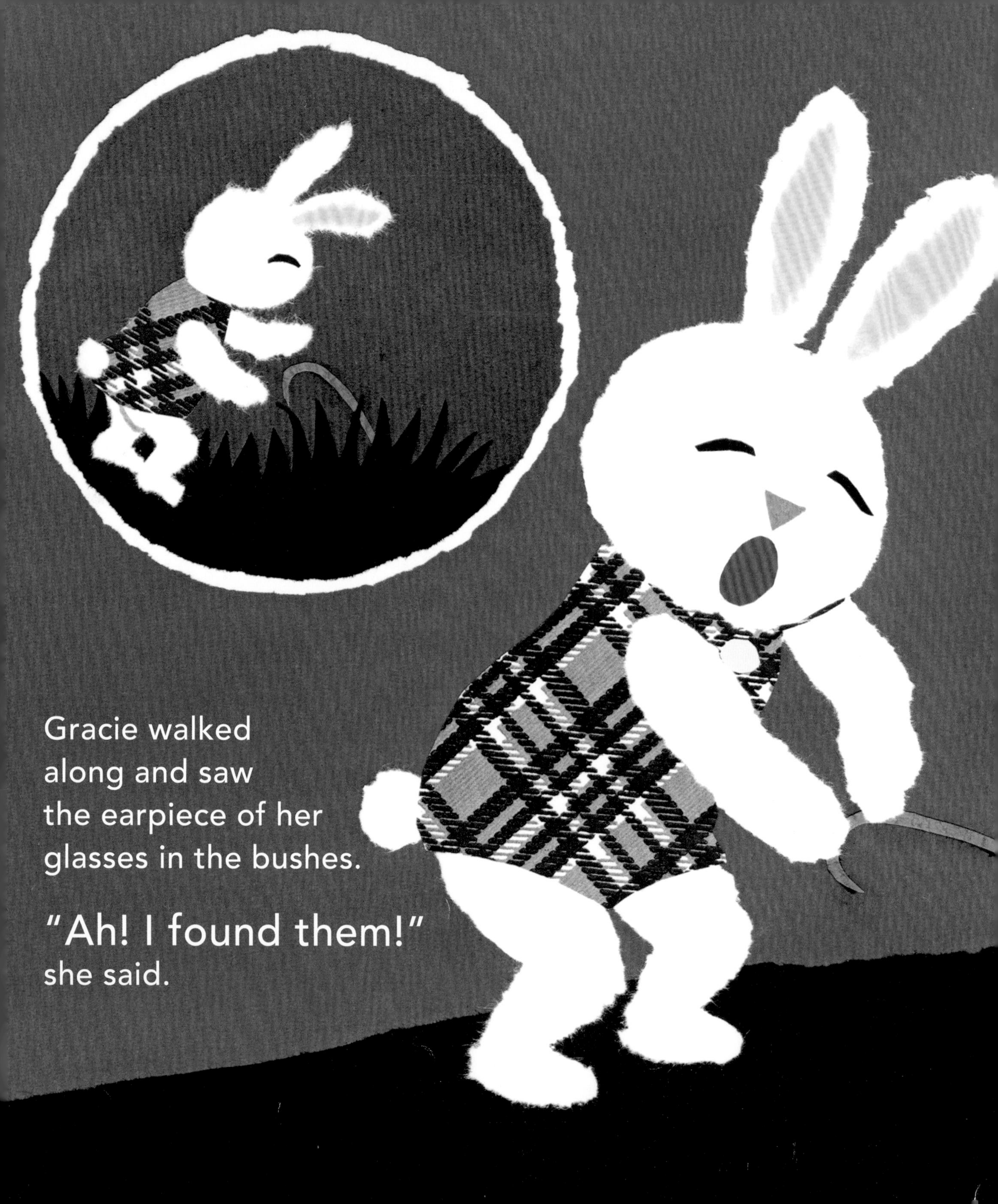

Gracie walked
along and saw
the earpiece of her
glasses in the bushes.

"Ah! I found them!"
she said.

"Ouch! Don't pull!" squeaked someone.

It was a mouse! What had looked like Gracie's glasses was really the mouse's tail.

"I'm so sorry! I thought that was my glasses," said Gracie.

"What a foolish bunny!" said the angry mouse.

Maybe I dropped my glasses in the woods, thought Gracie.

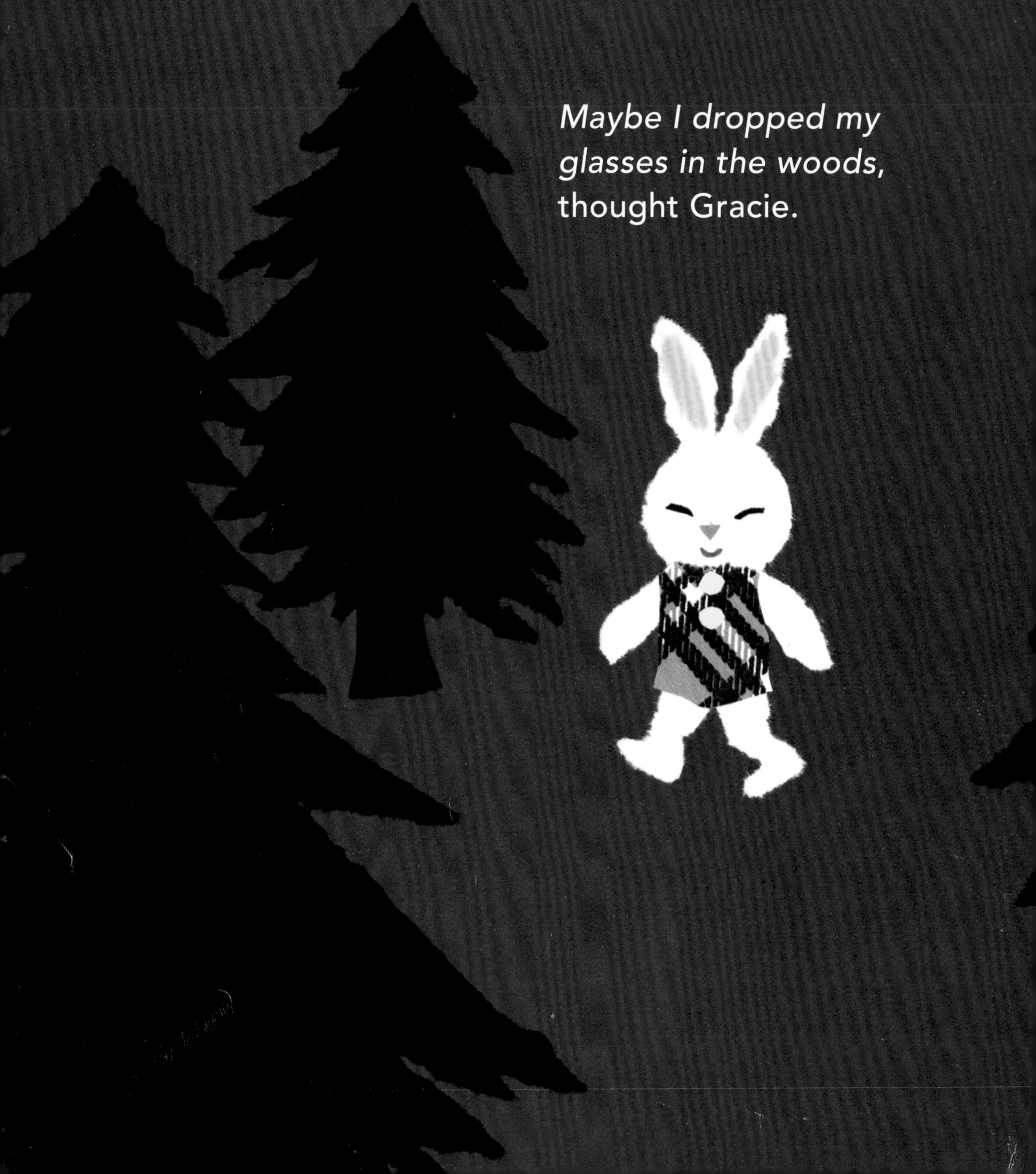

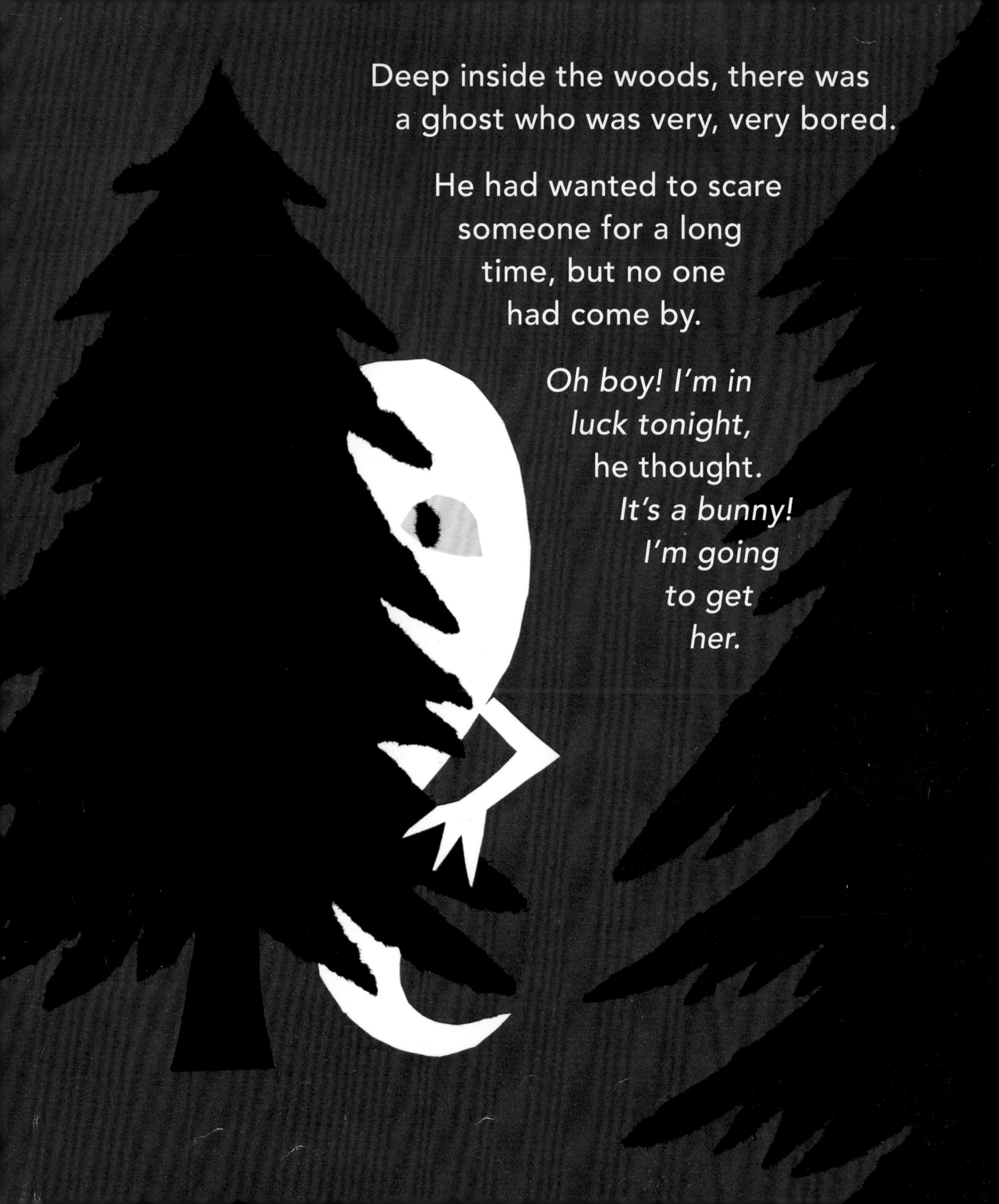

Deep inside the woods, there was
a ghost who was very, very bored.

He had wanted to scare
someone for a long
time, but no one
had come by.

*Oh boy! I'm in
luck tonight,*
he thought.
*It's a bunny!
I'm going
to get
her.*

The excited ghost jumped out and yelled,

"BOO!!"

But without her glasses Gracie couldn't see what was happening.

"What is that? Is it a balloon? Is it a sheet flapping in the wind?" she asked.

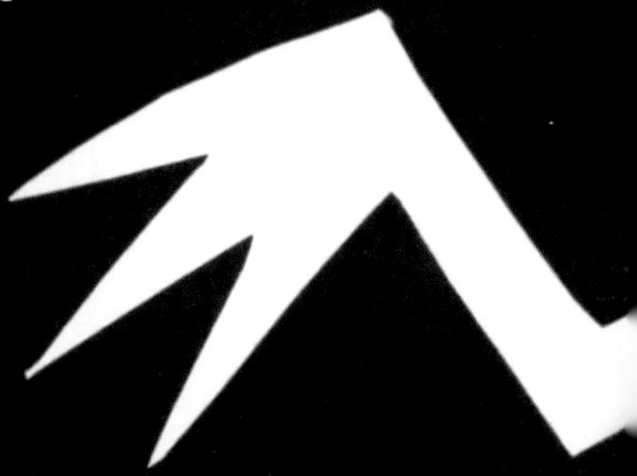

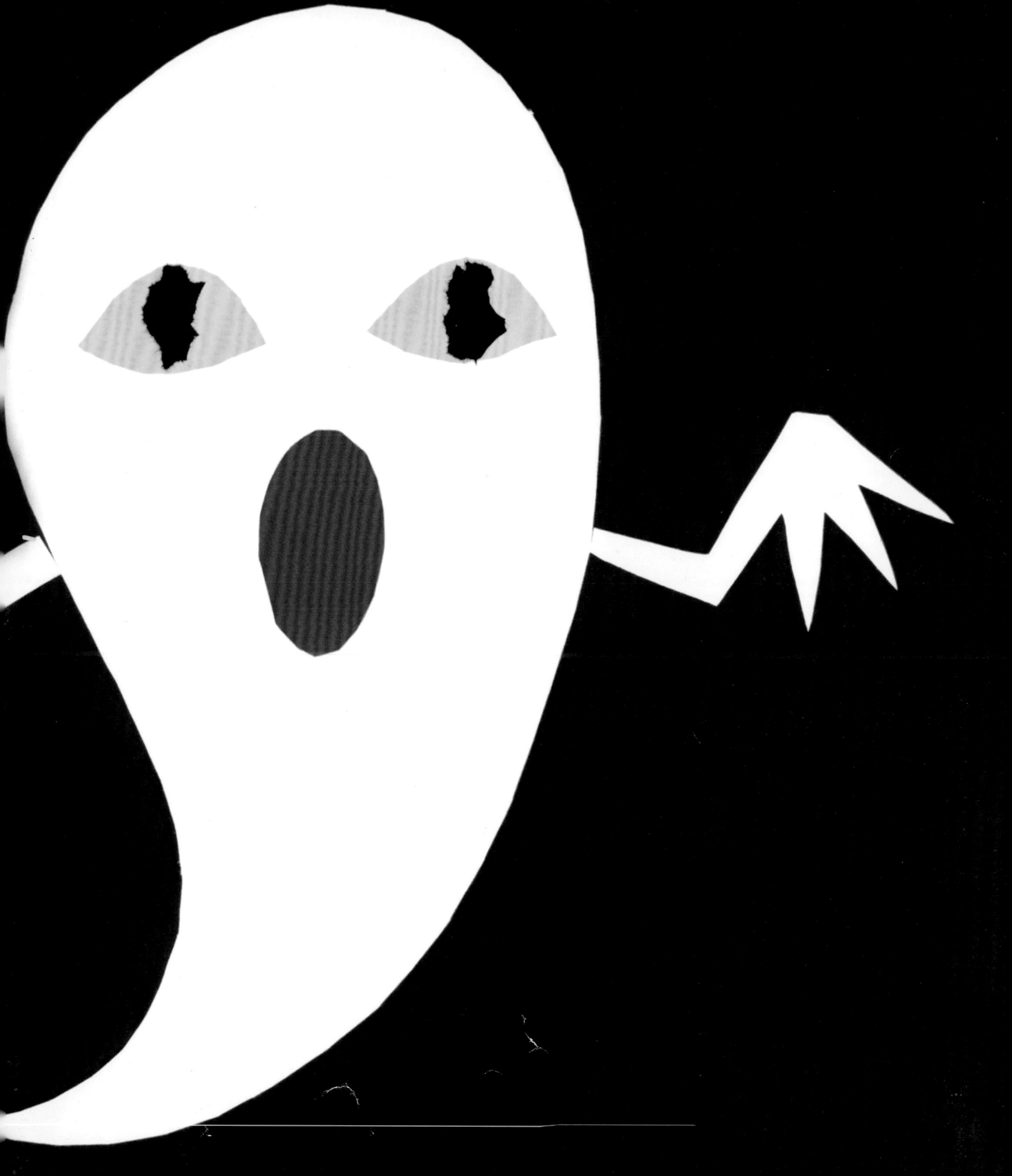

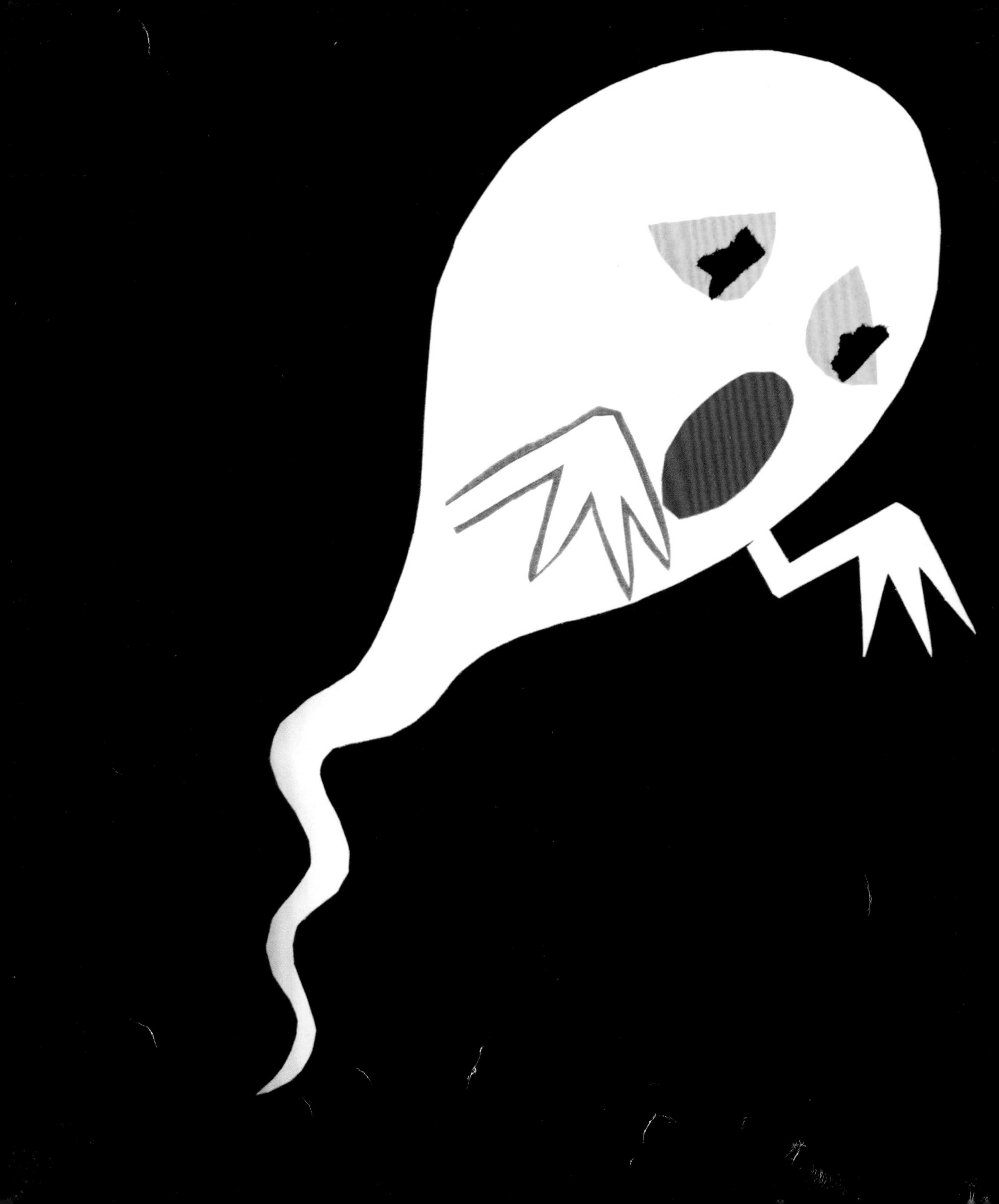

The ghost was disappointed.
"Hey, aren't you scared of me?"

"No. I can't see well because I lost my glasses.
I've come to look for them."

"Well, that explains it," said the ghost.
"If I help you find your glasses, will you put
them on and look at me?"

"Okay," said Gracie.

The ghost looked everywhere
for Gracie's glasses.

I don't know who he is,
but he's so kind and helpful,
Gracie thought, as she sat
under a tree and rested.

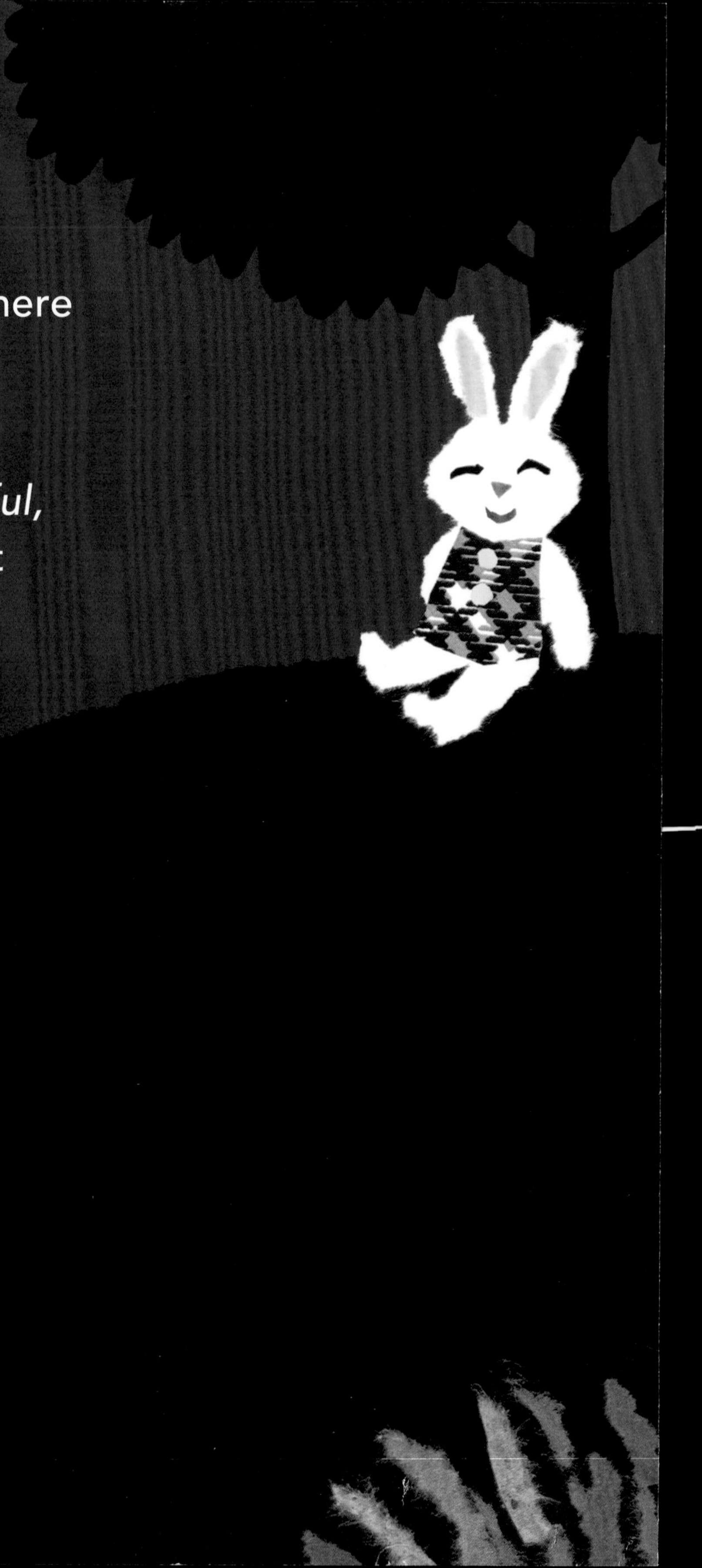

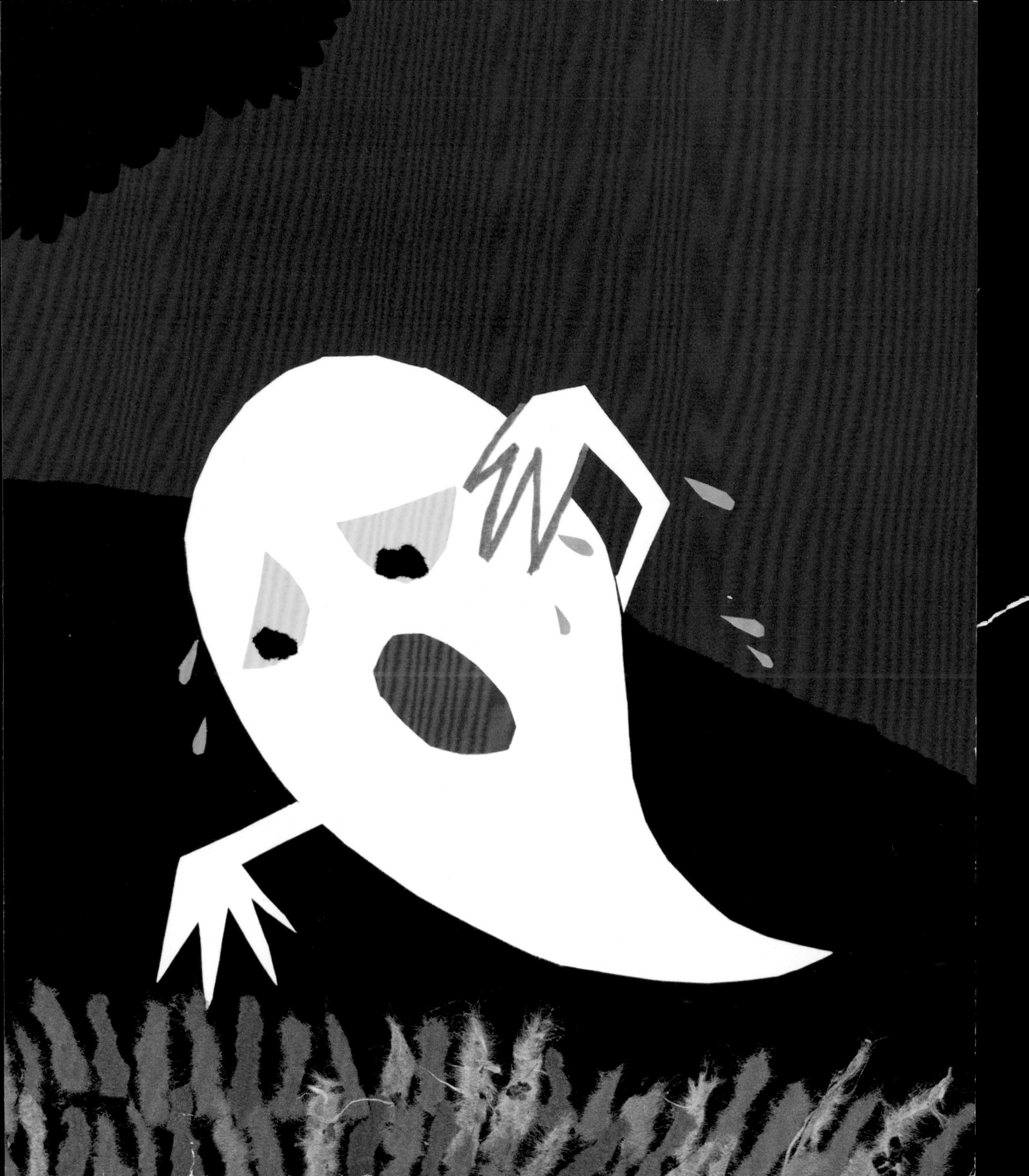

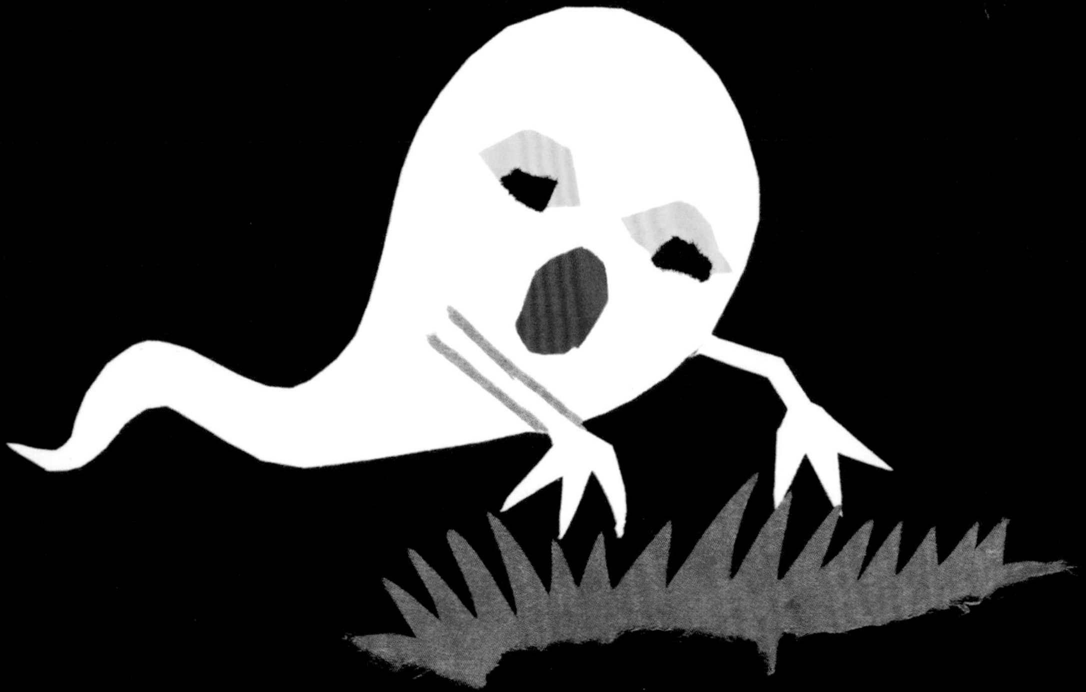

It was not easy to find the glasses. The ghost worked so hard that he was all in a sweat!

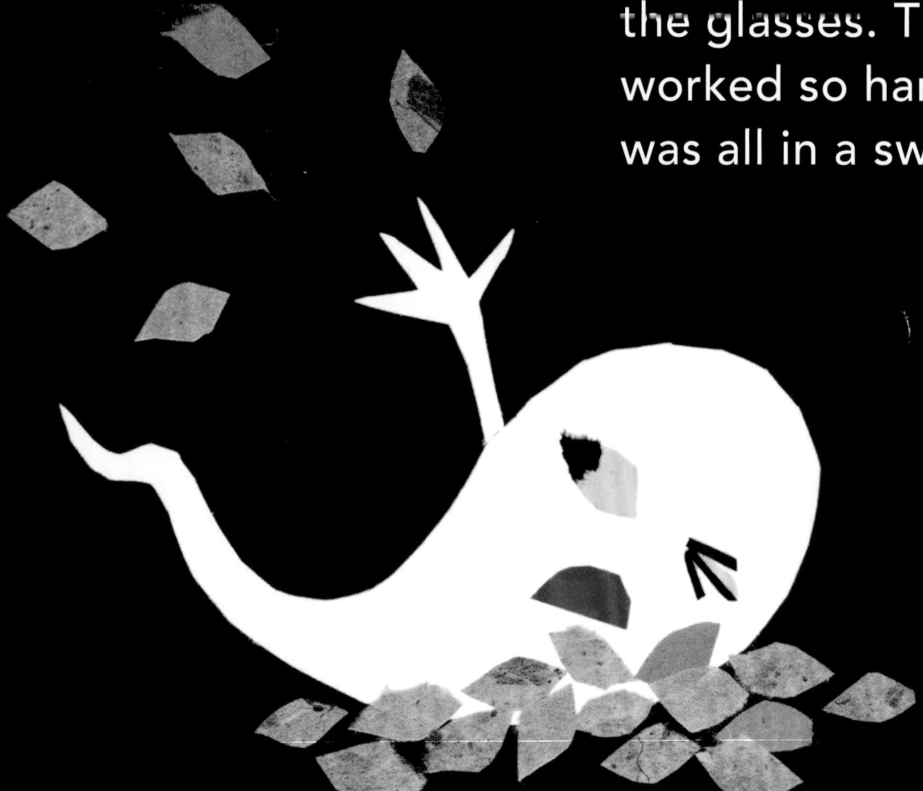

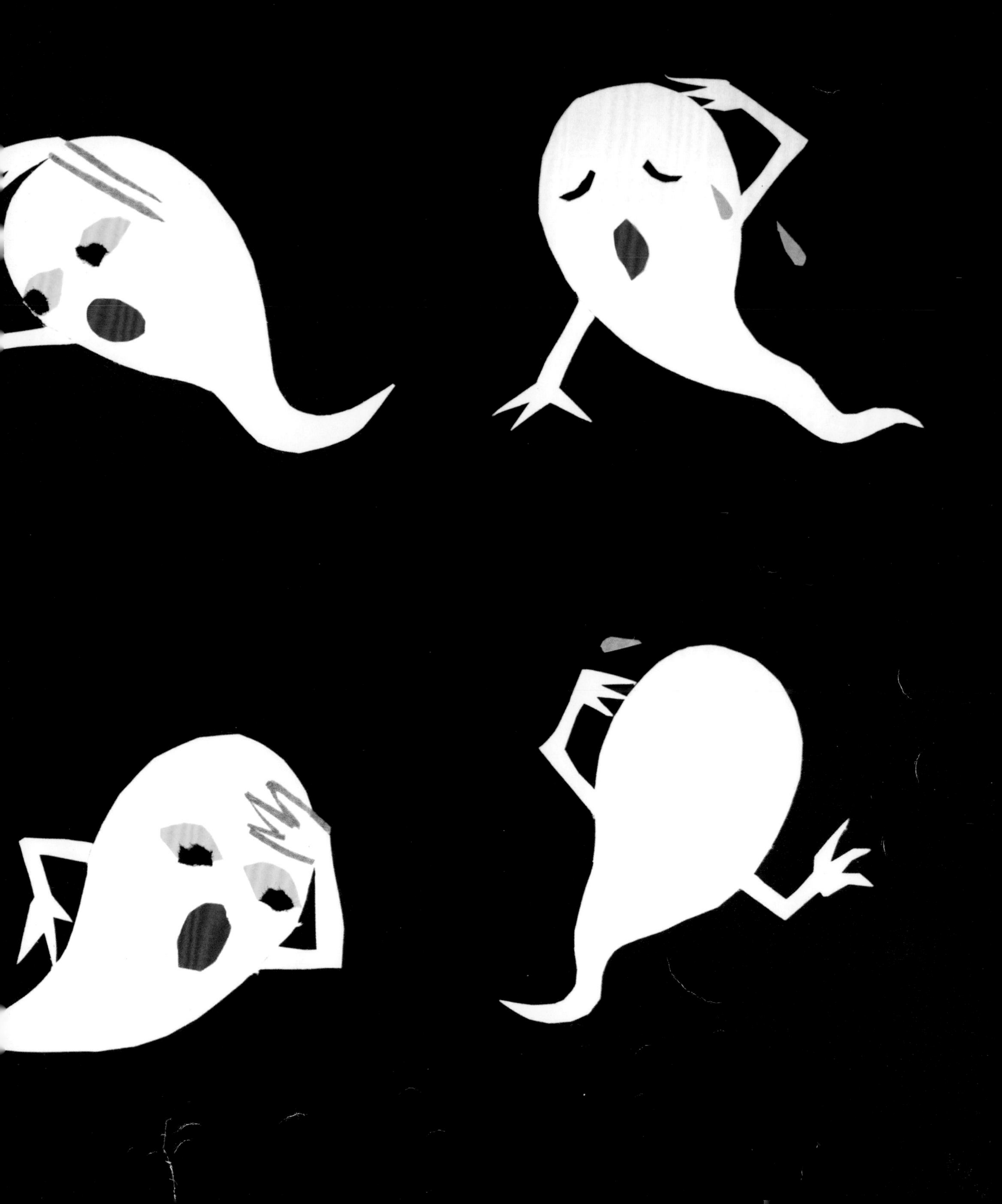

After searching all night, he finally saw Gracie's glasses.

"Ah! I found them!"

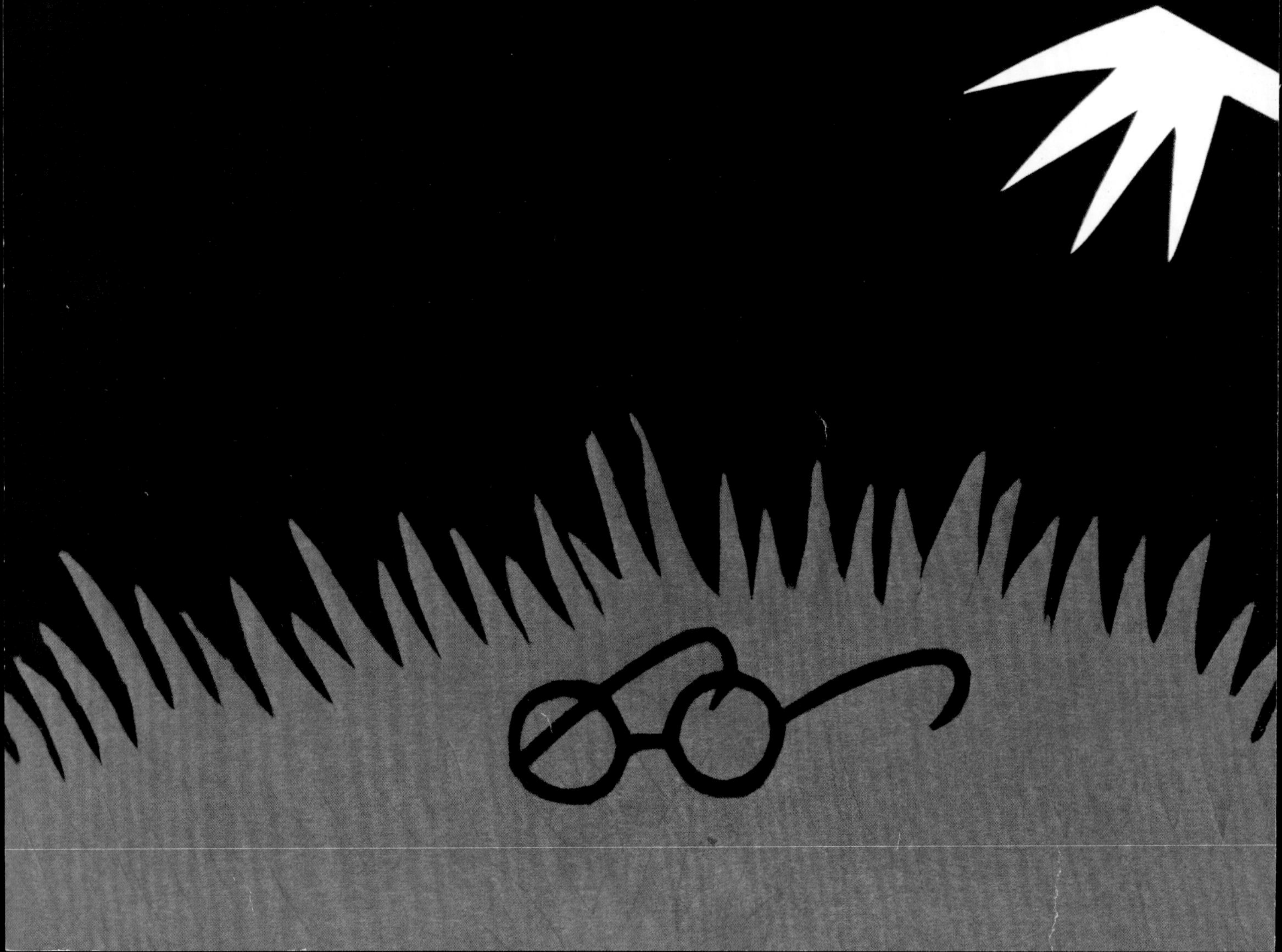

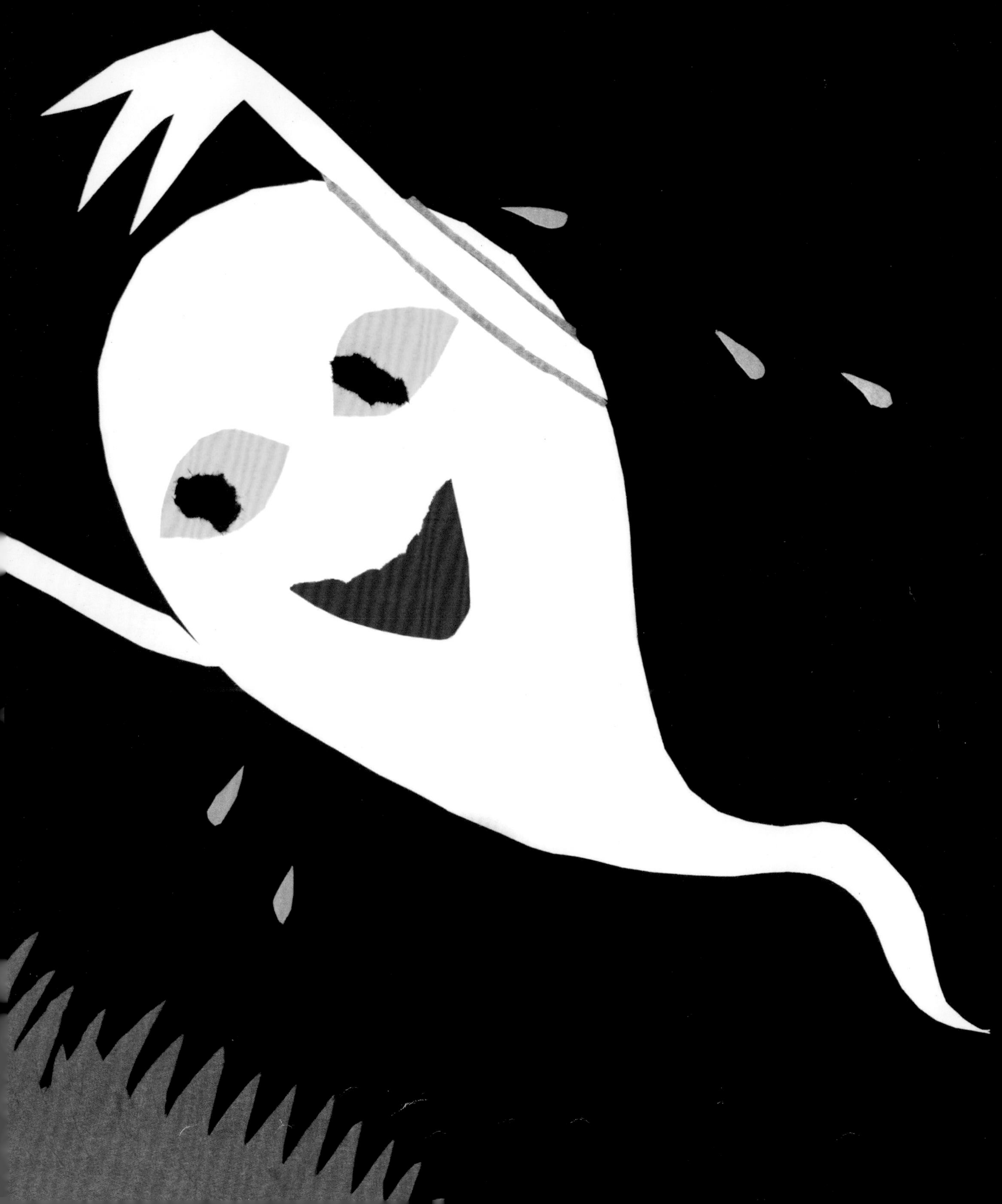

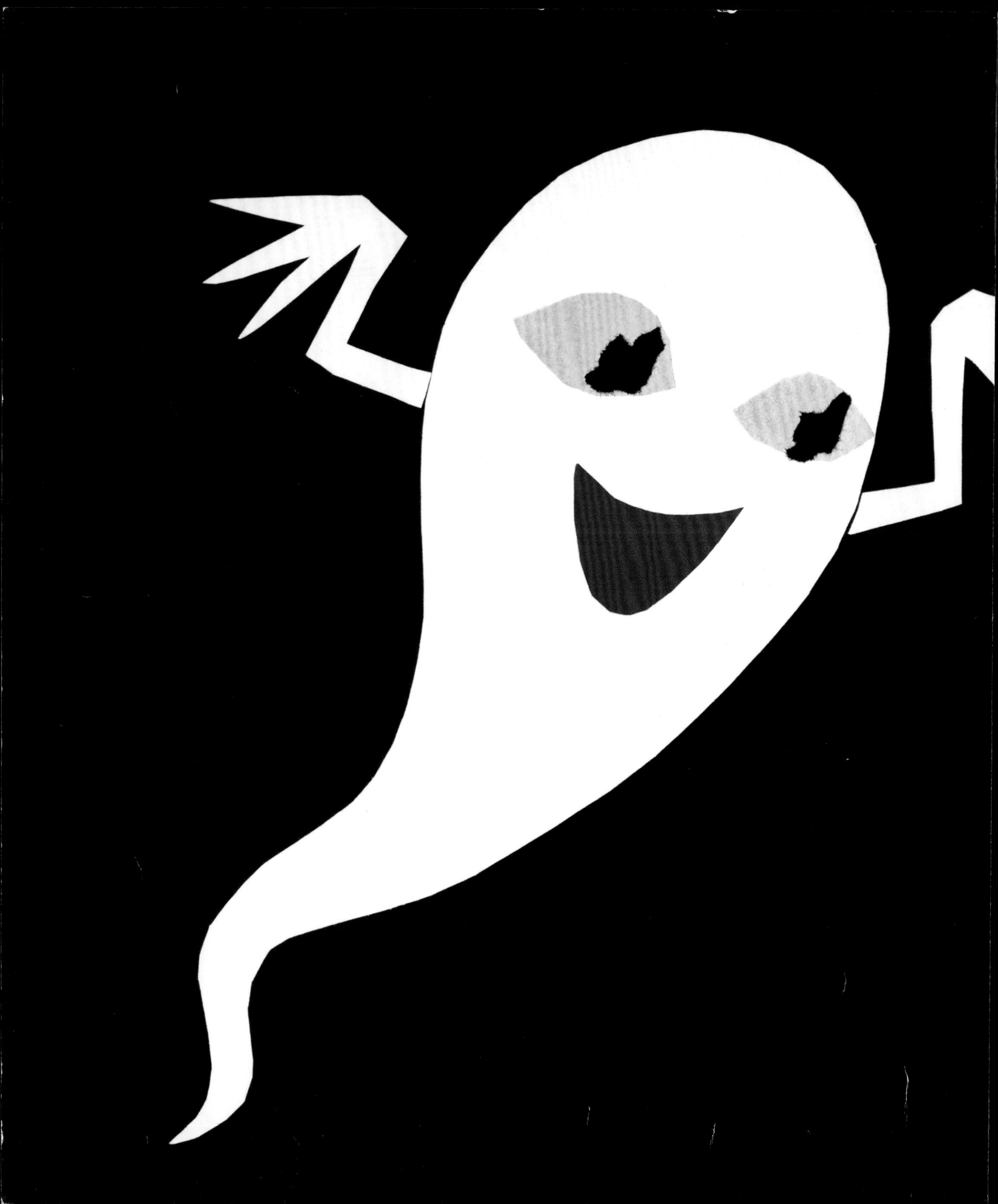

"Here you go. Now, put them on and look right at me."

He was sure that when Gracie saw him, she would scream and run away.

The ghost made himself as big as he could and was about to yell, "BOO!!" when . . .

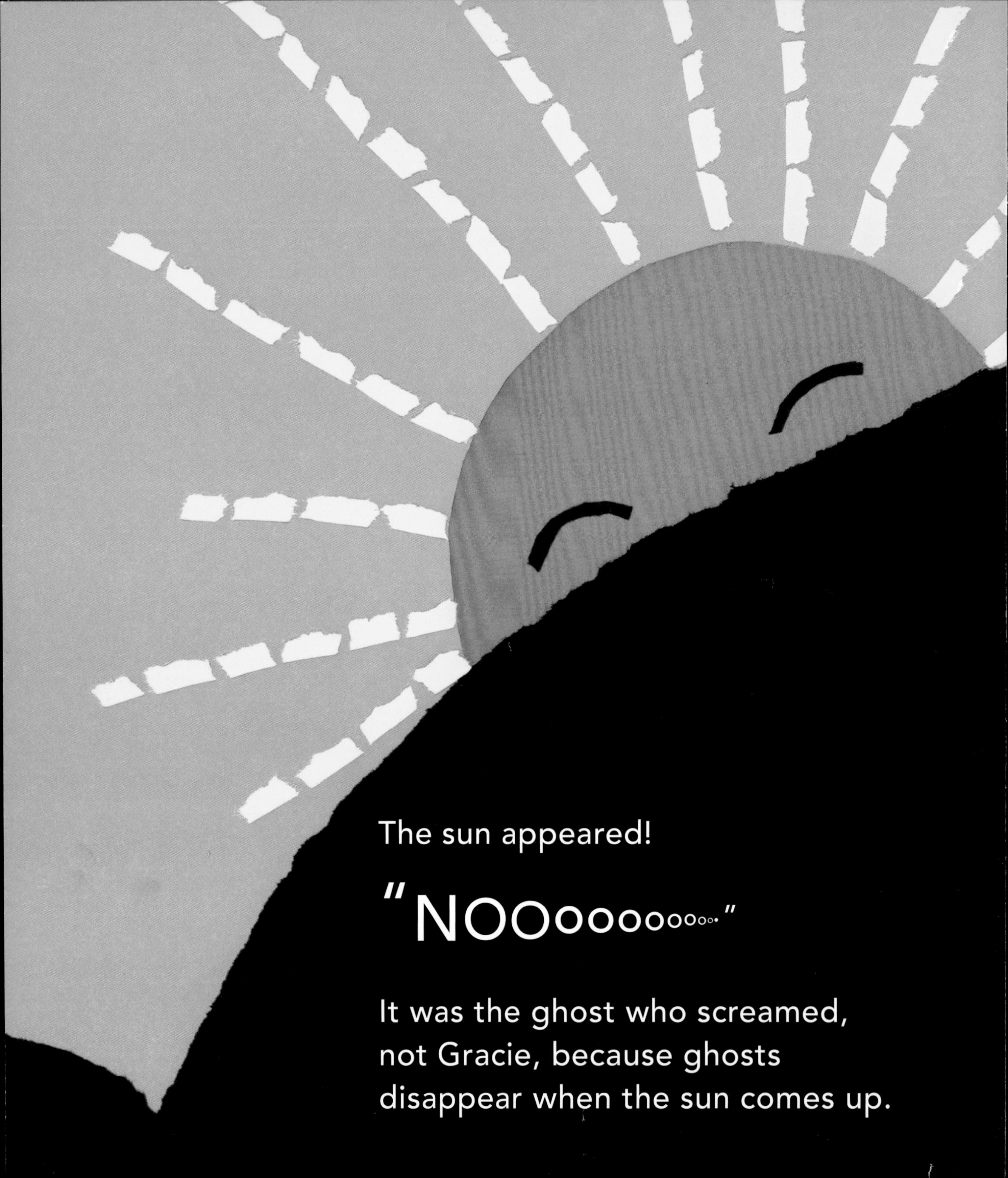

The sun appeared!

"NOOoooooooo."

It was the ghost who screamed, not Gracie, because ghosts disappear when the sun comes up.

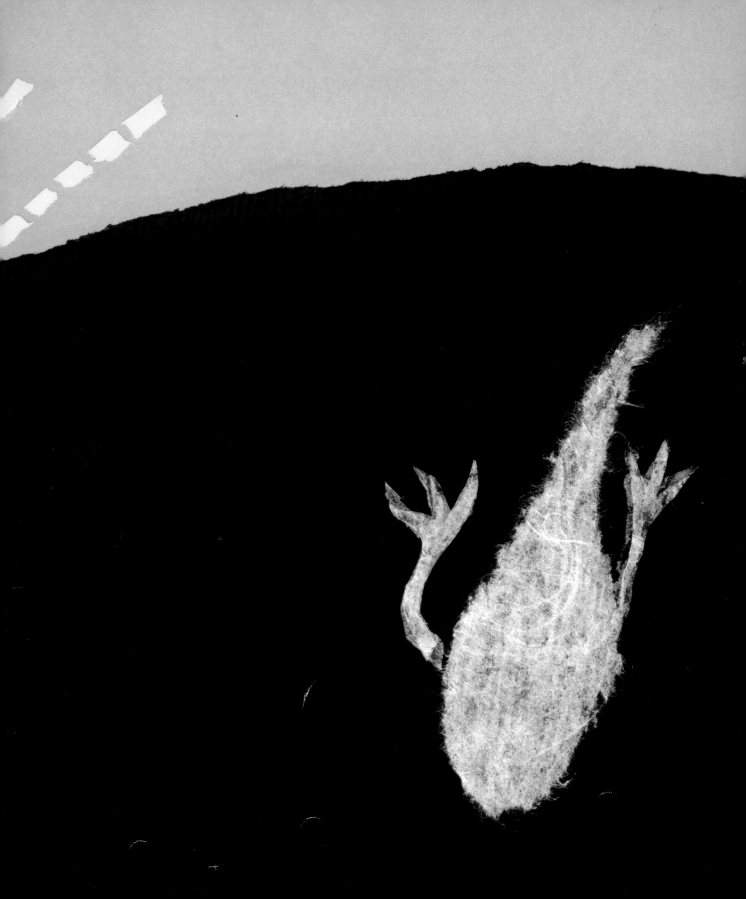

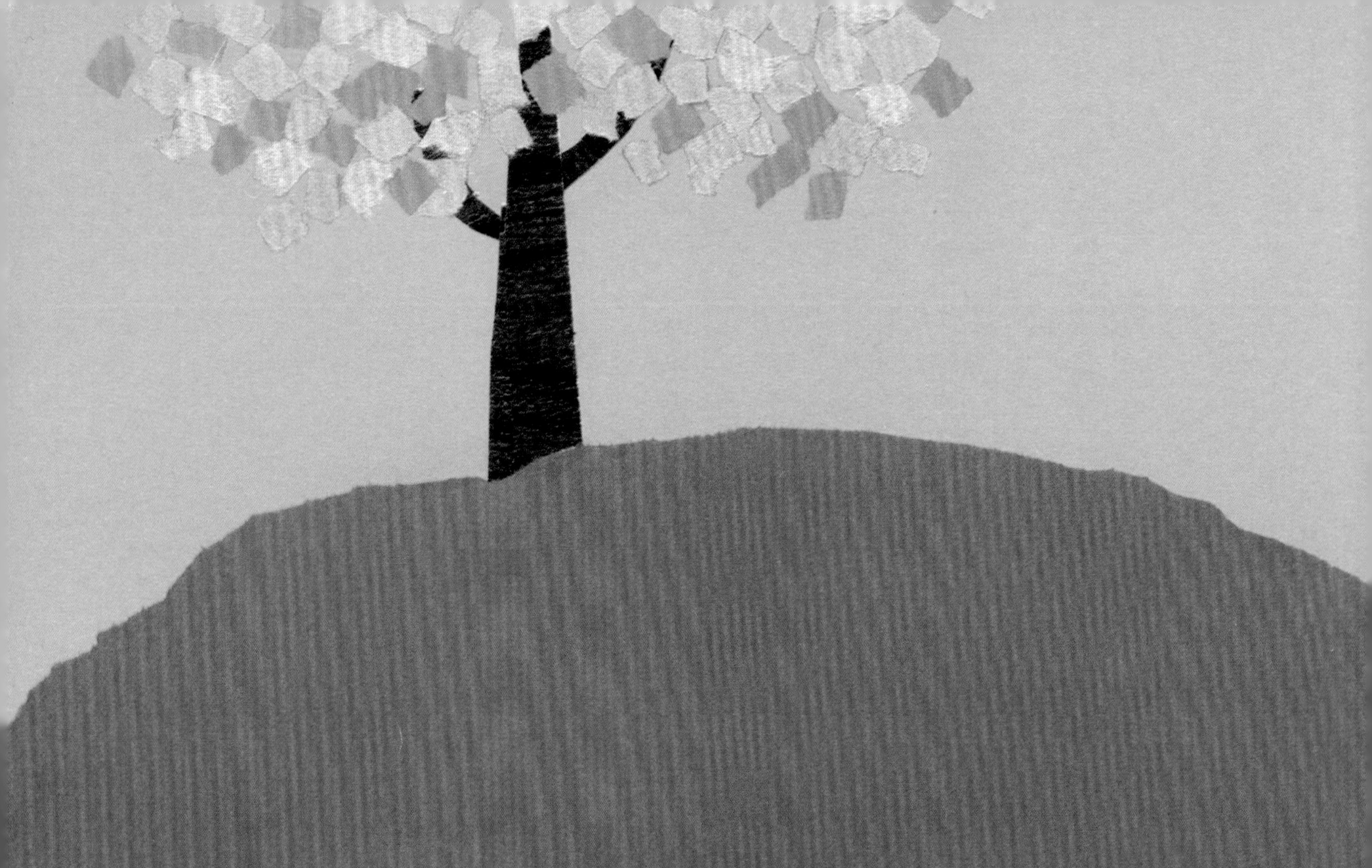

Gracie put on her glasses.

Where has that kind person gone?
she wondered. *I was very lucky to meet him.*
Oh well, I'll thank him if I see him again.

Then Gracie went home happily.
She never found out what happened!

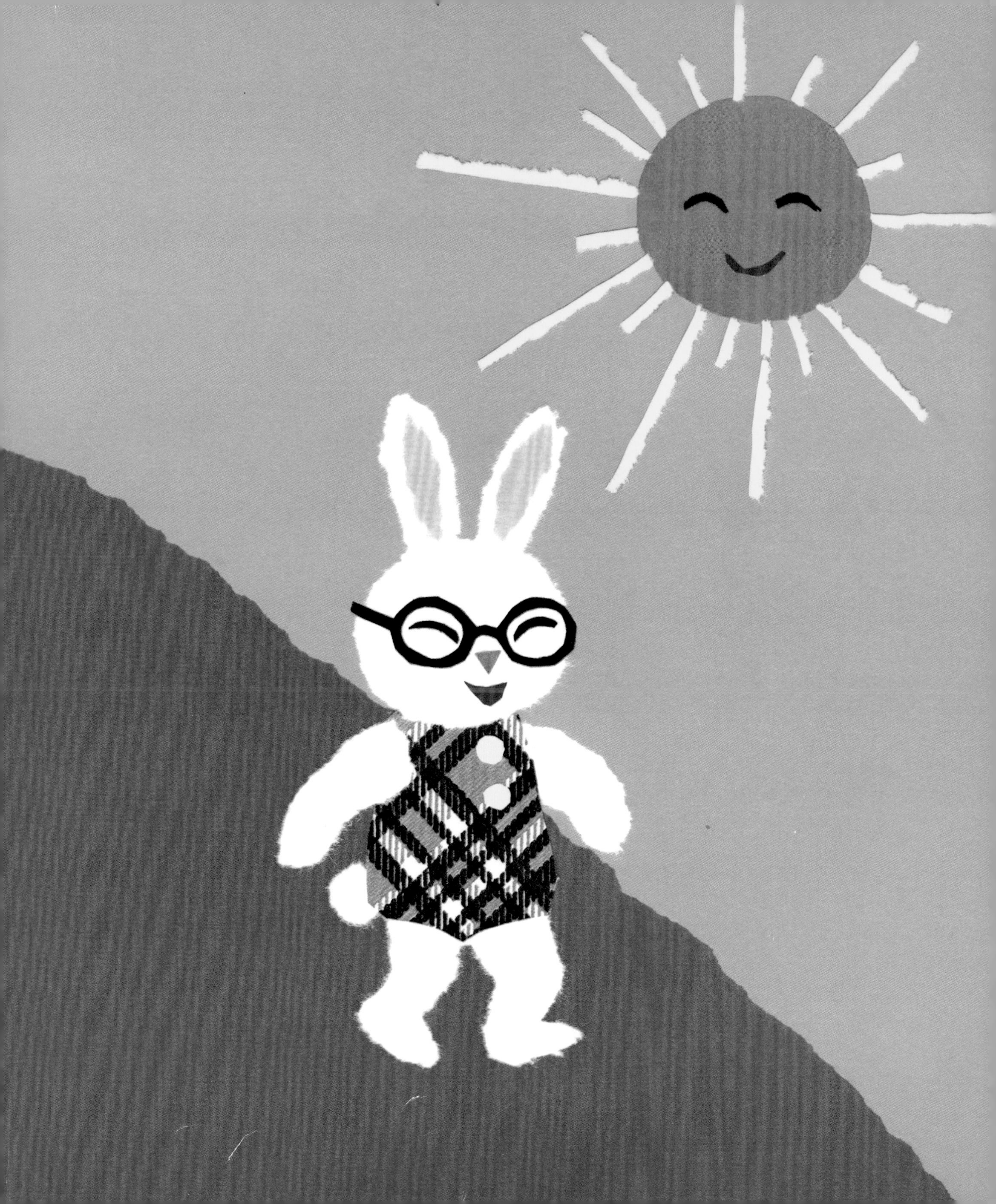

GRACIE MEETS A GHOST

Megane Usagi © 1975 Keiko Sena
All rights reserved.

Translation by Mariko Shii Gharbi
English editing by Simone Kaplan

Published in the United States and Canada by:
Museyon Inc.
1177 Avenue of the Americas, 5th Floor
New York, NY 10036

Museyon is a registered trademark.
Visit us online at www.museyon.com

Originally published in Japan in 1975 by POPLAR Publishing Co., Ltd.
English translation rights arranged with POPLAR Publishing Co., Ltd.

Printed in China

ISBN 978-1-940842-13-4